Not So Tall for Six

Dianna Hutts Aston

Illustrated by Frank W. Dormer

iii Charlesbridge

To Kelly Shelts and her Grandpa Mark—D. H. A.

For Victoria—F. W. D.

Text copyright © 2008 by Dianna Hutts Aston
Illustrations copyright © 2008 by Frank W. Dormer

Published by Charlesbridge
85 Main Street
Watertown, MA 02472
(617) 926-0329
www.charlesbridge.com

Library of Congress Cataloging-in-Publication Data
Aston, Dianna Hutts.
   Not so tall for six / Dianna Hutts Aston ; illustrated by Frank W. Dormer.
      p. cm.
   Summary: Six-year-old Kylie Bell comes from a long line of not-so-tall people, but she remembers
the family motto—"Brave and smart and big at heart"—which helps her to treat the class bully with kindness.
   ISBN 978-1-57091-705-9 (reinforced for library use)
[1. Size—Fiction. 2. Bullies—Fiction. 3. Schools—Fiction. 4. Kindness—Fiction.] I. Dormer, Frank W., ill. II. Title.
PZ7.A8483Not 2008
[E]—dc22   2007002279

Printed in China
(hc) 10 9 8 7 6 5 4 3 2 1

Illustrations done in pen and ink and watercolor on 140-lb. cold-press Winsor and Newton paper
Display type and text type set in Linotype Humana
Color separations by Chroma Graphics, Singapore
Printed and bound in China by Everbest Printing Company, Ltd., through Four Colour Imports, Ltd., Louisville, Kentucky
Production supervision by Brian G. Walker
Designed by Susan Mallory Sherman

Kylie Bell is small for six.

"Yep, the not-so-tallest one in first grade," she says, matter-of-factly.

Kylie Bell comes from a long line of not-so-tall people. But the Bell family has never let size get them down. Nope. The Bell family motto is "Brave and smart and big at heart."

Still, it's not so easy to reach the water fountain when your legs aren't much longer than rulers.

It's downright difficult to know what's ahead when everyone else is a head taller.

And it's nigh impossible to see the sky with that new bully-boy Rusty Jacks slithering around like a half-starved rattlesnake.

S

Kylie Bell is brave. Her daddy says she gets her courage from Great-uncle Fergus "Fangs" Bell, infamous snake charmer of the tall-grass prairie.

She opens her mouth to tell that Rusty Jacks
to go rattle his tail somewhere else, please.

But Rusty Jacks is lightning-quick. "Hissssss!"
he hisses, and Kylie Bell skedaddles faster than
a spooked horse.

At times like this a sneaky thought tip-tippity-two-steps across Kylie Bell's brain. She is so tall, the ground rumbles like a mighty oil gusher when she runs. She is so tee-totally-tall, big kids can play hopscotch in her shadow.

She is so positively giraffelike, she gets a permanent crick in her neck from looking down at the tops of her friends' heads. *Sigh.*

But Kylie Bell is not a moper. Nope, not a moper, nor a pouter, nor a whiner. Kylie Bell is, above all, a proud member of the Bell family.

On the playground Kylie Bell lightly leapfrogs over her classmates, but then that mean ol' Rusty Jacks comes along with his ol' bullfrog legs.

"Run for the swamp, Rusty Jacks!" Kylie Bell says. "Or my granny'll fry up a batch of frog legs for supper. Yours!"

For a split second Rusty Jacks looks like a fear-frozen jackrabbit.

Then he skulks away, squawking,
"Tastes like chicken!"

Kylie Bell organizes a new game—piggyback races. Everyone wants Kylie Bell to be their piggy, because she's the lightest.

Suddenly, a thunderhead blots out the sun. *Uh oh.* That's no cloud.

"Hey, little bug," Rusty says to Kylie Bell. "I'll give you a piggyback ride."

"No, thank you!" Kylie Bell says.

"You afraid?" he says.

Gulp.

"Kylie Bell is a *ladybug*, a little-bitty, itsy-witsy *'fraidy-bug,*" he sings in his singin'-meanie voice.

Kylie Bell *is* afraid. But even though her legs feel like Aunt Cherokee's cactus jelly, she skitter-dee-doos over to Rusty Jacks, looks straight up into his nostrils, and announces, "Ladybugs do *not* accept rides from wild boars."

"Ladybug," Rusty Jacks snickers. "'Fraidy-bug!
Lady-lady-'fraidy-bug!"

For one brief, shining moment, Kylie Bell imagines him
as a rhinoceros beetle, fearsomely creepy and shunned by all . . .
and she almost calls him such. But a vision of Great-great-
grandmother Beulah Bell, who kept hold of her good manners
even when the cowpokes didn't, pops into her mind.

Kylie Bell takes two ladylike, rhino-sized breaths and says, "I may not be so tall for six, but I have good manners. I am very polite for six."

And when Rusty Jacks doubles in size, Kylie Bell sprints for safety—a move she learned from Big Brother Bubba Bell—and hollers, "I may not be so tall for six, but I have fast feet. I am very fast for six!"

In the classroom, everyone breaks into literary circles. Everyone but Rusty Jacks. None of them—not the Beavers nor the Bison nor the Ponies—want that big ol' meanie in their circle.

"Circle leaders?" Ms. Shelts calls. "Who has a spot for Rusty?"

Kylie Bell squirms, trying hard to ignore the question. A hush as big as an elephant fills the room. A flush of pink creeps up Rusty Jacks's neck. Kylie Bell can't ignore that little Bell voice bizzity-buzzing around in her head like a pesky gnat, telling her what she already knows. Brave and smart and big at heart. *Sigh.*

Kylie Bell takes two ladylike, rhino-sized breaths and says, "We do. The Shetland Ponies have a spot for Rusty Jacks in our circle."

"Thank you, Kylie," says Ms. Shelts.

Slowly, like a praying mantis, Rusty Jacks stalks toward Kylie Bell's group. His shadow falls across the circle. Kylie Bell squeezes her eyes shut tight against visions of chomped-up ladybugs.

Then, that mean ol' Rusty Jacks sits—ker-*splat!*—beside Kylie Bell. He puts his face right up to hers and says, . . .

Thanks, Ladybug.

Kylie Bell almost tells Rusty Jacks that there are boy
ladybugs too, but she doesn't. Instead, she says, "This is
my favorite book of all time. I hope you like it."

And later, for one brief shining moment, Kylie Bell
looks down and sees the tops of everyone's heads.
The ground rumbles as she moves forward. Then she
leans over, way, way over . . .

. . . that big ol' softie Rusty Jacks for a drink of water.